C903246518

For Alkandros and Sofia xx

M.R.

For Ivo and Iggy,

With love xx

R.B.

EGMONT

We bring stories to life

First published in Great Britain 2019
by Egmont UK Limited,
The Yellow Building, 1 Nicholas Road, London W11 4AN
www.egmont.co.uk

Text copyright © Michelle Robinson 2019
Illustrations copyright © Rosalind Beardshaw 2019

Michelle Robinson and Rosalind Beardshaw have asserted their moral rights.

ISBN 978 1 4052 8864 4

A CIP catalogue record for this title is available from the British Library.

1, 2, 3, Do the Dinosaur

Michelle Robinson

Rosalind Beardshaw

EGMONT

It started long ago in
the middle of the jungle.

The ground began to **jiggle** and to **wriggle** and to **rumble** . . .

A dinosaur called Tom tapped a rhythm on a tree
And he beckoned all his buddies, shouting,
"Come and copy me!"

He stood up on his tiptoes

and he

slashed

his giant claws.

"Now, open wide," he shouted, "let's all chomp our dino jaws!

Chomp, **chomp**, chomp!
Let's do the dinosaur!
One, two, three and . . .
everybody ROAR!"

He arched his spiky back and then he shook his shiny scales.
"Now sway your hips,"
he ordered.

"Show me how you
swish your tails!

Swish,
swish,
swish!

Let's do the dinosaur!
One, two, three and . . .

everybody ROAR!"

"You're looking good," said Tom,

"but tell me, can you
stomp around?"

He lifted up
his feet and
crashed
them loudly on the ground!

"Stomp, stomp, stomp!
Let's do the dinosaur!
One, two, three and . . .
everybody ROAR!"

The little one said, "Quiet, Tom.
We're making quite a din."

Tom paused. "You're right," he whispered.

Then he added with a grin . . .

"Let's do it really quietly!
We'll take it from the top.

We'll **chomp** and **swish** and **stomp** and . . .

Uh oh!

Everybody . . .

stop!"

The little one said,
"Run for it!"

and all the dinos hid.

They said, "D'you think he saw us?"
and Tom answered, "He **SO** did!"

What's all this dancing for?

Can I try joining in as well?"

Tom frowned . . .

then shouted . . .

"Sure! Just copy all the actions and you'll quickly know the score!

You **chomp**

and **swish**

and **stomp** about, and **that's** the dinosaur!

Chomp, swish, stomp!

Let's do the dinosaur!

One, two, three and . . .

everybody
ROAR!"

The little one was sleepy now. "Me, too," the T. rex said.

"Then everybody copy me," said Tom . . .

"It's time for bed!

Yawn, yawn, yawn!

We've done the dinosaur.

One, two, three and . . .